For my husband Jim, thank you for your love and encouragement.

For my grandchildren, my inspiration, Michael, Emma, Sadie, Kailee, Court, Natalie, Cody, Taylor, Cecilia, and Dominick.

www.mascotbooks.com

Odonata: The Flying Jewel of Maiden Grass Pond

For more information, please contact:
Mascot Books
560 Herndon Parkway #120
Herndon, VA 20170
info@mascotbooks.com

Library of Congress Control Number: 2017910183

CPSIA Code: PBANG0917A
ISBN-13: 978-1-68401-349-4

Printed in the United States

ODONATA

The Flying Jewel
of Maiden Grass Pond

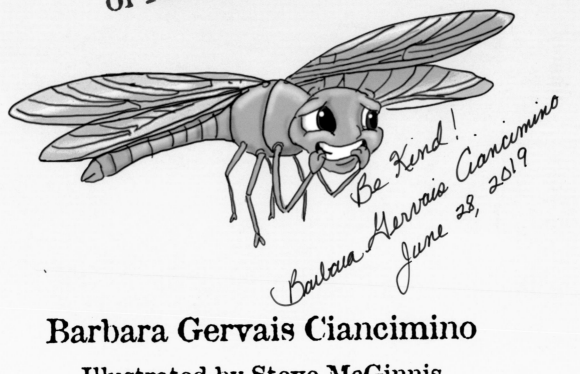

Be Kind!
Barbara Gervais Ciancimino
June 28, 2019

Barbara Gervais Ciancimino

Illustrated by Steve McGinnis

Odonata was a dragonfly who didn't look like the other dragonflies living on Maiden Grass Pond. He didn't have blue and green iridescent wings like they did. His wings were colorless and dull.

None of the dragonflies wanted to be his friend. They didn't like that he looked different. Every time Odonata tried to play with them, they ignored him and pretended he was not there.

There was, however, one dragonfly who didn't ignore Odonata. His name was Drago. He was a humongous Blue Hawker dragonfly who did mean and despicable things to the insects living around the pond, especially Odonata.

"Hey! Odo-no-color, where did you get those hideous wings?" Drago would call out. Then, without warning, he would fly right toward Odonata, trying to knock him into the dangerous water below.

A new day brought an overcast sky and rainy weather to Maiden Grass Pond. The rain clouds made Odonata's wings look grayer and duller than usual, but they also gave him a good reason to stay hidden among the reeds and away from Drago.

Odonata knew how dangerous it was for dragonflies to fly in the rain. If a dragonfly got its wings wet, it would fall from the sky into the perilous water below, or worse, into the hungry mouth of Croaker the bullfrog, who was perched on his lily pad, waiting for a snack.

Odonata watched from a distance as the other dragonflies finished up their game of tag. They were chasing each other playfully around the pond, when suddenly,

BAM!

Drago crashed right into the middle of them, sending dragonflies tumbling in all directions! They were upset with Drago, but none of them had the courage to say anything to him. Then, as the last dragonfly managed to straighten its wings, the rain began to fall.

Everyone quickly darted into the Maiden Grass to get out of the rain. Everyone, except Drago.

Showing off as usual, Drago flew straight up into the rain clouds. Odonata and the others watched and waited for Drago to return. The rain began to come down harder.

Something must be wrong, thought Odonata. *He should have come back by now. Where could he be?*

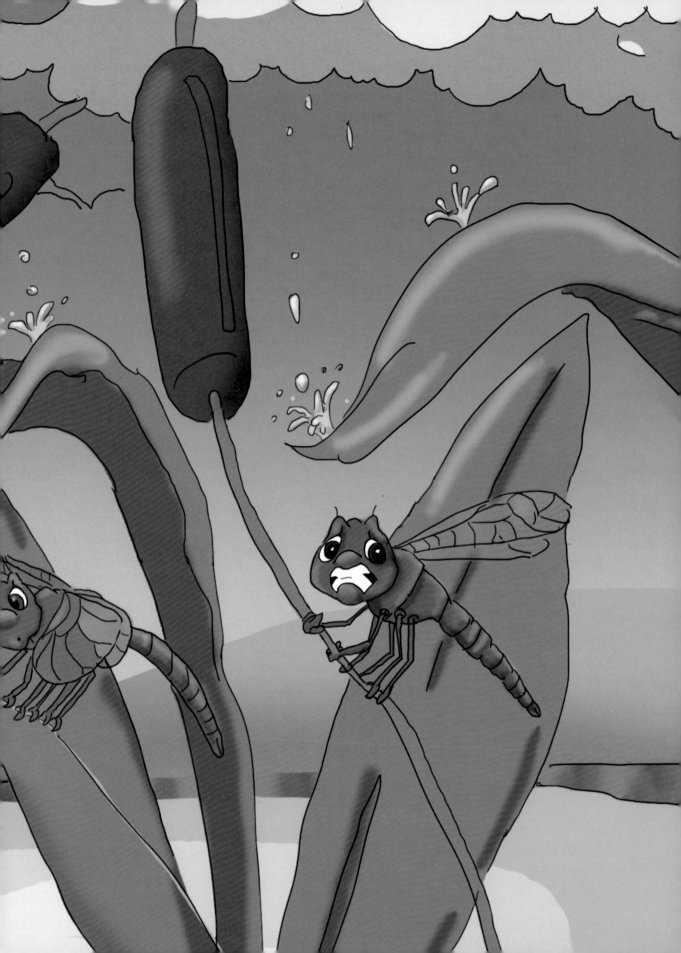

Then something incredible happened. Odonata spread his colorless wings, flew out of the reeds, through the rain, and up toward the clouds.

The other dragonflies watched in horror. Surely, Odonata's wings would get drenched with rain, and he would fall helplessly into Maiden Grass Pond and become a tasty meal for Croaker the bullfrog.

But Odonata was only thinking of one thing: saving Drago. He flew higher and higher, until he reached the edge of the storm. Odonata hesitated for a second, closed his eyes, and flew into the ominous storm clouds.

Once on the other side, Odonata opened his eyes. There was a colorful mist all around him. The sun's rays were shining through the falling raindrops, creating tiny, multicolored prisms in the air. He was inside the most magnificent rainbow he had ever seen.

Odonata flew through the many colors
of the rainbow searching and calling out to
Drago. There was no sign of him.

Odonata stopped to rest on the edge of the
yellow mizzle. While clinging there on the
fringe of the rainbow, he thought he heard his
name. He looked around and there, huddled
on the bottom of the blue mist, was Drago.

"How did you know where I was?" asked Drago.

"I saw you fly up toward the rain clouds," said Odonata.

"But how were you able to fly in the rain?" Drago asked, confused. "My wings are soaked through."

Odonata could not answer him. He didn't know how he was able to fly in the rain, but he knew what he had to do next.

"Climb onto my back and hold on," said Odonata. "Let's get you out of here."

The rain had finally stopped, but Drago
continued to cling to Odonata. He was still too
weak to fly on his own. Slowly, the two of them
made their way back to Maiden Grass Pond.

The other dragonflies were gathering below. They could not believe it. Odonata had put his own life in danger to save Drago, even though he had been so mean to him.

As soon as Odonata landed and Drago slid off his back, the dragonflies flew over to them. Then a strange thing happened. **"LOOK AT YOUR WINGS!"** gasped Drago.

Odonata brought his wings forward to look at them. He was speechless. His wings looked like majestic stained glass windows, painted with the radiant colors of the rainbow. They were the grandest wings he had ever seen.

As the dragonflies admired Odonata's new wings, Drago touched his wing to Odonata's to thank him for saving his life. Then, he apologized to everyone for being so unkind and promised to never be mean again.

Odonata never did figure out how he was able to fly in the rain or how his wings became so radiant. But he knew he was happier than he had ever been, spending his days playing with Drago and the other dragonflies.

One sunny afternoon, as Drago and Odonata were flying around the pond, Drago called out, "Hey, Odonata, where did you get those sparkling wings? They make you look like a flying jewel gliding in the sunshine." Odonata smiled.

From that day forward, Odonata was known as the Flying Jewel of Maiden Grass Pond.

THE
END

20 FUN FACTS ABOUT DRAGONFLIES

- A dragonfly is an insect that belongs to the scientific order Odonata, which means "toothed one."

- There are 5,900 different species of dragonflies.

- Dragonflies have been on the Earth for more than 300 million years.

- Dragonflies live near ponds and streams.

- A female dragonfly lays her eggs on a plant in the water.

- Baby dragonflies, or larva, hatch from eggs underwater.

- As larva, baby dragonflies feed on water insects, tiny fish, and sometimes tadpoles.

- A dragonfly larva slowly changes into an adult dragonfly.

- Dragonflies have excellent eyesight, with two large compound eyes that have 30,000 individual facets, more than any other insect.

- Dragonflies have ultra-color vision, allowing them to see clearer and in more colors than any other animal in the animal kingdom.

- Dragonflies cannot fly in the rain.

- Dragonflies eat insects.

- Dragonflies dart around grabbing insects with their feet.

- Dragonflies hover like helicopters over the water to catch insects.

- Dragonflies eat hundreds of mosquitoes every day.

- The Blue Hawker dragonfly, or darner, is the largest dragonfly in North America.

- Blue Hawker dragonflies fight and crash into intruder dragonflies, sending them spinning through the air.

- The Blue Hawker is a curious dragonfly and will fly close to people to check them out.

- Dragonflies do not bite or sting.

- Dragonflies, sometimes known as "sewing needles," do not sew up the mouths of naughty children.

ABOUT THE AUTHOR

Barbara is a retired elementary school teacher who lives in New England with her husband, Jim, and their dog, Ty. Together, they have five children and ten grandchildren, who are the inspiration for her writing. She was born and raised in the city of Hartford, Connecticut, where she later spent twenty-four years teaching reading, writing, and science. Still a teacher at heart, Barbara enjoys incorporating scientific facts about her characters into her stories.

Barbara graduated magna cum laude from Central Connecticut State University with a Master's Degree in Elementary Education. She has been a member of SCBWI since 2015.

One of Barbara's talents is baking and creating character and wedding cakes for friends and family. She also loves having adventures with her grandchildren and spending time at the beach with her family.